This book belongs to:

_____

A catalogue record for this book is available from the British Library
Published by Ladybird Books Ltd
80 Strand London WC2R 0RL
A Penguin Company
2 4 6 8 10 9 7 5 3 1
© Ladybird Books Ltd MMVI. This edition MMVIII

ISBN: 978-1-84646-977-0
Printed in China

# Dick
# Whittington

Retold by Vera Southgate M.A., B.Com
with illustrations by David Kearney

Ladybird *tales*

Once upon a time, there was a poor boy who was called Dick Whittington. His mother and father were dead and he had no one to care for him.

Dick lived in a small village in the country. He tried to work for his living but he could not always find work to do.

Dick was very poor. His clothes were thin and ragged and sometimes he had very little to eat.

In those days people did not often travel far from the village in which they lived. Dick's village was a long way from London.

When the village people talked of London, they spoke of it as a wonderful place. They said that all the people in the city of London were rich. They even said that the streets of London were paved with gold.

Dick listened to these tales and he longed to go to London.

Dick thought that if he went to London he would be able to pick up gold from the streets. Then he would become rich and need never feel cold or hungry again.

Dick made up his mind to go to London, although he had no idea how far it was. He made his few clothes into a bundle and tied the bundle to the end of his stick. Then he set off to walk along the road to London.

Dick walked a long way but he did not reach London. Just as he was beginning to feel very tired, a hay cart came along the road.

The driver stopped the cart and said to Dick, "Where are you going, my lad?"

"I'm going to London, sir," replied Dick.

"Then jump up beside me," said the driver, "and I'll take you to London."

When they drove into the city of London, Dick gazed about him in wonder.

First, he was very surprised to see how many people there were in the streets. He had never seen so many people before, in all his life.
He was also amazed to see all the fine churches, shops and houses.

When Dick had got over his first wonderment, he began to look for the streets that were paved with gold. Nowhere could he find them.

It grew dark and Dick was tired and hungry. He had nowhere to sleep, so he curled up in a doorway and went to sleep there.

Next morning Dick tried to find work for himself. He walked along street after street, asking people for work, but no one had a job to offer him.

When night came, Dick was so weak from hunger and tiredness that he sank down on the nearest doorstep.

Now it happened that this house belonged to a rich man, named Mr Fitzwarren. He was a merchant who made his money by selling things to people in other countries.

Mr Fitzwarren's cook found Dick on the doorstep and was angry. "You lazy boy," she cried. "What are you doing there? Get up from my master's doorstep!"

Poor Dick tried to rise, but he was too weak. At that very moment, Mr Fitzwarren himself arrived home.

Mr Fitzwarren was a kind-hearted man. He spoke gently to Dick and listened to his story.

"If it's work you want," he said, "you can work in my house, for my cook. You will have plenty to eat and a bed to sleep in."

Dick was so happy that he could hardly find words with which to thank Mr Fitzwarren.

Dick's happiness did not last long. He soon found that the cook was an unkind woman. She was always scolding him and sometimes she used to beat him.

Mr Fitzwarren had a daughter named Alice. She was kind, like her father, and she knew that the cook was cruel to Dick. Alice took pity on Dick and forbade the cook to hit him.

This made things easier for Dick, although he still had to work very hard.

Dick's bed was in a cold attic at the top of the house. This attic was overrun with rats and mice. At night, as Dick tried to sleep, the rats and mice ran over his bed. He could not rest.

"If only I had a cat," thought Dick, "she would be a friend to me and she would chase away the rats and mice."

But all the money that Dick had in the world was one penny.

Next day, Dick went to the market with his penny in his pocket. There he saw a woman holding a cat in her arms.

"Please will you sell me your cat?" Dick asked the woman.

"I'm not sure that I want to sell her," said the woman. "She's a grand cat for catching mice."

"That's just what I need," said Dick. He pleaded so hard that at last the woman agreed to sell him her cat for a penny.

From that day, Dick's life became happier. He loved his cat and looked upon her as his friend. At night he slept well because his cat chased away all the rats and mice.

Now, Mr Fitzwarren had many ships that sailed to distant lands.

One day, Mr Fitzwarren called all the servants together. He told them that one of his ships was ready to sail. Everyone was allowed to send something with the captain to be sold in a faraway country. That way, they could make some money.

"Do you want to send something on my ship?" Mr Fitzwarren asked Dick.

"I have nothing in the world except my cat," replied Dick.

"Then you must send your cat," said Alice.

Poor Dick did not really want to part with his cat, but, to please Alice, he agreed.

Dick missed his cat and wished he had never sent her away. Once more he could not sleep at night, because of the mice running over his bed.

Dick was so unhappy that he made up his mind to run away.

Early one morning, he crept out of the house before anyone was awake.

Dick had not gone far when the bells of Bow Church began to ring. The bells seemed to be singing this tune to Dick,

*"Turn again, Whittington,*
*Lord Mayor of London,*
*Turn again, Whittington,*
*Thrice Mayor of London."*

"If I am to be Lord Mayor of London," thought Dick, "I will turn again." So, before anyone missed him, he turned back to Mr Fitzwarren's house and let himself in.

Meanwhile, on the ship, Dick's cat was making herself very useful. The ship was overrun with rats and mice. Dick's cat was a fine rat-catcher and she soon killed hundreds of them.

After sailing for many weeks, the ship came to a far country. The king of the country invited the captain to come to the palace.

A wonderful meal was prepared for the king and queen and the captain.

Many servants carried in the food on gold and silver dishes, and set it in front of them. But before anyone could take a bite, hundreds of rats rushed into the room. The servants tried to drive them back with big sticks, but it was no use. In no time at all, the rats had eaten all the food.

The captain was astonished by this sight. He turned to the king and asked, "Why do you put up with these rats, Your Majesty?"

"There is nothing we can do about it," replied the king. "Every time we sit down to eat, it is the same. My wise men have tried to make spells, but they have not managed to get rid of the rats."

"Then why don't you have a cat?" asked the captain.

"A cat!" said the queen. "What is a cat?" So the captain described a cat. Then the king and queen told him that there was no such animal in their country.

"I would give half my kingdom for a cat!" said the king.

The captain went back to his ship, picked up Dick's cat and returned to the palace. He arrived just as a meal was being served.

The rats were beginning to eat the food on the gold and silver dishes. The cat jumped out of the captain's arms. She killed dozens of rats and the rest fled in fear.

The king and queen were astonished and delighted. "Oh, Captain! We must have that cat!" cried the queen.

The king agreed to buy Dick's cat. The queen asked to see what else the captain had for sale.

The sailors carried to the king's palace all the goods they had to sell. The king and queen bought everything.

For Dick's cat, the king paid ten times as much as he had paid for all the other things put together. He gave the captain a casket full of gold and jewels, in exchange for the cat.

When the ship got home, the captain went straight to Mr Fitzwarren and told him the news.

Mr Fitzwarren sent a servant to the kitchen saying, "Ask Mr Whittington to step up here, please." Dick thought the servant was making fun of him.

Mr Fitzwarren handed Dick the casket of jewels. "You are now a very rich man, Mr Whittington," he said. "Your cat has made your fortune."

Dick could hardly believe this good news. He thanked Mr Fitzwarren, and the captain, with all his heart.

Miss Alice was very happy to hear about Dick's good fortune. "First, you must buy yourself some new clothes," she said. Dick did so, and very smart he looked in them.

Dick was now a wealthy man. When he asked Mr Fitzwarren if he could marry his daughter, Alice, Mr Fitzwarren was glad to give his consent.

Some years later, Dick became Lord Mayor of London. Indeed, he was Lord Mayor of London three times.

So the Bow Bells had been right, when they said to him,

*"Turn again, Whittington,*
*Lord Mayor of London,*
*Turn again, Whittington,*
*Thrice Mayor of London."*

Beauty
and the
Beast

Ladybird tales

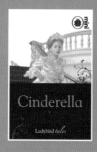

Cinderella

Ladybird tales

Hansel
and
Gretel

Ladybird tales

The Princess
and the Pea

Ladybird tales

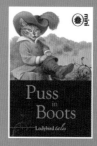

Puss
in
Boots

Ladybird tales

Sleeping
Beauty

Ladybird tales

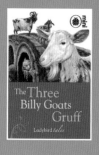

The Three
Billy Goats
Gruff

Ladybird tales

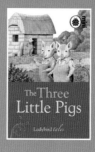

The Three
Little Pigs

Ladybird tales

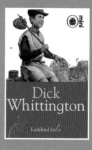

Dick
Whittington

Ladybird tales

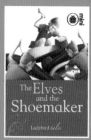

The Elves
and the
Shoemaker

Ladybird tales

The Little
Red Hen

Ladybird tales

Snow White
and the
Seven Dwarfs

Ladybird tales